Omnibus Books
An imprint of Scholastic Australia Pty Limited
PO Box 579 Gosford NSW 2250
ABN 11 000 614 577
www.scholastic.com.au

Part of the Scholastic Group
Sydney • Auckland • New York • Toronto • London • Mexico City
New Delhi • Hong Kong • Buenos Aires • Puerto Rico

Possum Magic Actions first published by Omnibus Books in 2015.

Possum Magic Opposites first published by Omnibus Books in 2012.

Possum Magic Numbers first published by Omnibus Books in 2012.

Possum Magic Colours first published by Omnibus Books in 2016.

This bind-up edition published by Omnibus Books in 2023.

NATIONAL LIBRARY OF AUSTRALIA
A catalogue record for this book is available from the National Library of Australia

ISBN: 978-1-76129-740-3

Julie Vivas used watercolour for the illustrations in this book.
Cover design by Nicole Stofberg.

Printed in China by RR Donnelley.
Scholastic Australia's policy, in association with RR Donnelley, is to use papers that are renewable and made efficiently with wood from responsibly managed sources, so as to minimise its environmental footprint.

10 9 8 7 6 5 4 3 2 1 23 24 25 26 27 / 2

MY FIRST BOOK OF POSSUM MAGIC

Written by
Mem Fox

Illustrated by
Julie Vivas

An Omnibus Book from Scholastic Australia

Possum Magic
Actions

eating

drinking

reading

thinking

smiling

singing

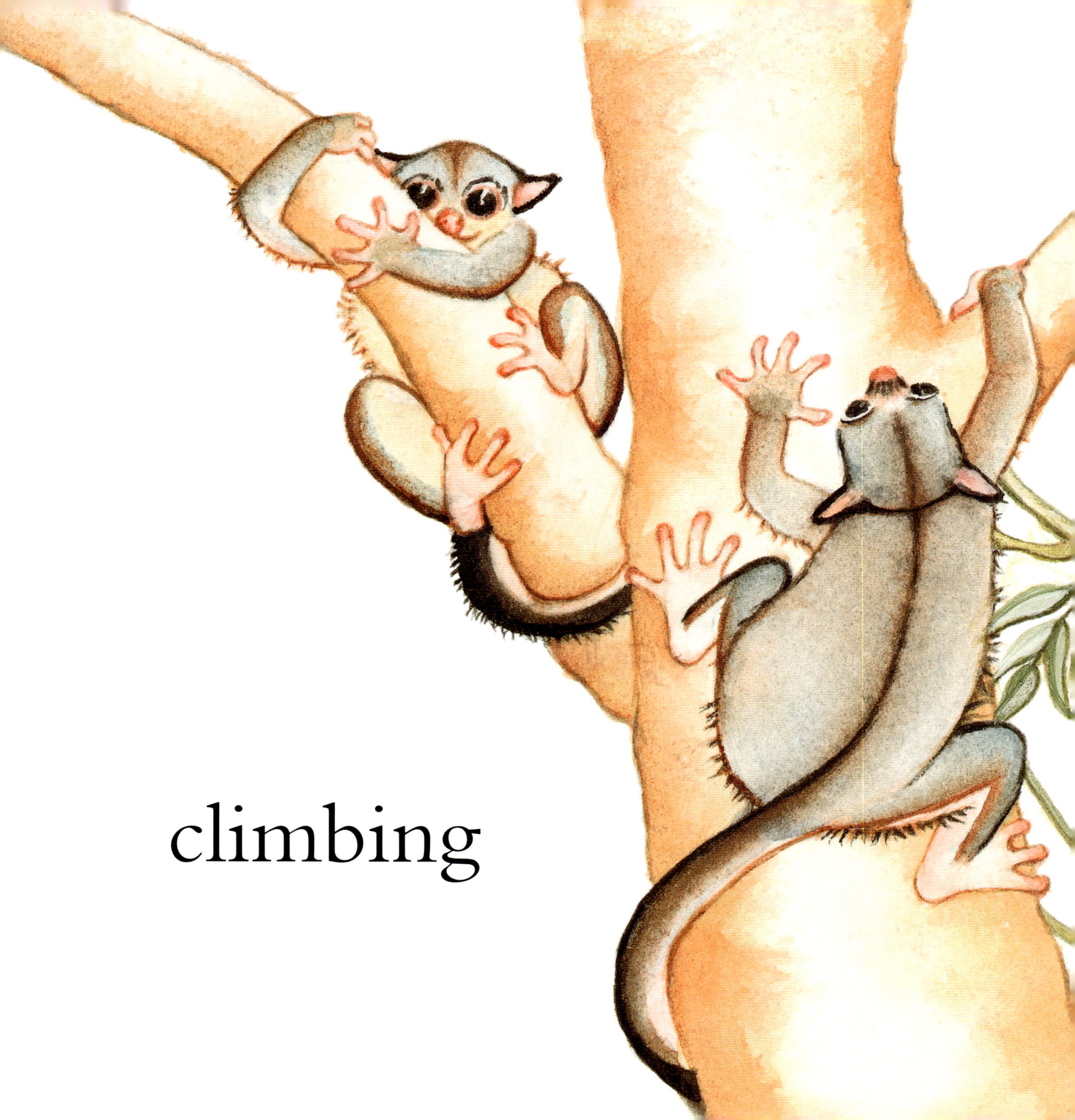

climbing

swinging

jumping

running

hiding

riding

sailing

dancing

Possum Magic
Opposites

tall

small

up

down

curly

straight

square

round

dirty

clean

spiky

smooth

awake

asleep

Possum Magic
Numbers

one possum

two kookaburras

three koalas

four umbrellas

five tails

six slippers

seven leaves

eight blossoms

nine lamingtons

ten bites

lots and lots of stars!

Possum Magic

Colours

blue

brown

grey

orange

pink

green

red

yellow